Joy Ride

A Reluctant Feminization and T-girl Suspense Romance

This book is dedicated to my fur baby, Snuggles.

He passed away on August 28, 2022.

Thank you for giving me 15 years and 3
months of unconditional love.

I will always love you.

Not to forget, YOU. The mere fact that you're
about to read this means that

you're part of the reason why I am blessed
to have a decent job amidst the

lack of opportunities for women like me in my country.

Thank you, from the bottom of my pink and girly heart <3

A Book By

LILLY LUSTWOOD

Table of Contents

Introduction

" It was just the two of them, chased by the police, not knowing how far they'd go… in short shorts and a long blonde wig "

Brian Bacall was celebrating his last month in Nevada before moving to Harvard Law School. As he regained consciousness from drowning in whiskey and margaritas, he decided to go home.

Treading the back alley of the club, he stumbled upon a harrowing scene that would introduce him to Honey Jones and a new life as a fugitive in short shorts and high heels.

Clutch your Pearl Necklace Tight and

Prepare for a Transgender Romance Ride!

Note: This title contains feminization, transgender romance, suspense, drama, and first time with a transgender woman tropes. Some real places and people were referenced but the story is a work of fiction. The cover image is from DepositPhotos and Lilly Lustwood.

I'm Lilly Lustwood and I'm a transgender woman. I'm a senior editor by day and I recall and write my romantic rendezvous by night.

Most of my titles deal with feminization. A fragment of what makes me find happiness in my gender identity, amidst the discrimination against women like me is my transformation.

When I look in the mirror and I gaze at my authentic self, I know that no matter what happens, I'm living my life and not somebody else's idea of how I should.

The clothes I wear, my long black hair, the fruity bath products that I use, the hormone medications I take before I go to bed, the sillage of my floral perfume, the surgeries I've undergone, and every step that I take with my size 12 Jimmy Choos, are all proudly from me...

…from my authentic feminine self.

Picture this…

- ✓ I have long and straight black hair and stand 5ft 6in.
- ✓ My alabaster curvaceous physique enjoys silk dresses
- ✓ I'm blessed with huge cat eyes and heart-shaped lips
- ✓ My friends tell me that I look like Haifa Wehbe, Google her
- ✓ I want to share the rest but that's not very lady-like *wink*

It's December 17, 2022, and 03:22 PM in the Philippines. It's scalding and I'm wearing a pink tube top and white hot pants.

Now that you know what your storyteller looks like, let's get to Joy Ride.

Before we get to the exciting part, I'm cordially inviting you to be a Lilly Lustwood VIP.

IT DOESN'T COST ANYTHING. All you have to do is Join my Mailing List.

I will be sending you FREE Exclusive Romantic Content that you won't find anywhere else.

My First Gift for You

Apart from that, I'll also send you Announcements of my New Releases and Promos.

I won't send you anything that's not related to my stories and I won't share your information with any person or entity.

CLICK TO READ FOR FREE

or Copy this Link -> stats.sender.net/

forms/er756a/view

Note: Please check your Spam or Promotions tab
if the confirmation doesn't arrive in your inbox.

Love Always,

Lilly

Chapter 1

It was past two in the morning and the *Electro Heat* club in Las Vegas was still popping. Amidst the thumping speakers and the crowd's noise, there wasn't anything audible enough to disturb 25-year-old Brian Bacall's drunken slumber.

He got into the club too early, just before nine in the evening with his friends Mike and John and both of them have abandoned him to spend emotionless romps at the place of the girls they just met the same evening.

As he suffered the repercussions of an abundance of whiskey and margaritas in one of the tables of the club's VIP room that was decked in black leather and red modernity, a muffled illicit exchange was happening just at the club's backdoor alley.

There she was, Honey Jones, a transgender brunette bombshell who stood 5ft. 9in. in three-inch heeled boots. As she chewed her gum and drew her lighter out of her cropped leather jacket's pocket, a brute Puerto Rican middle-aged man in a red lumberjack ensemble approached her with a light.

As he lusted at the view of her oppressive hips and butt in black leather short shorts, she gave him a look that she meant business. With a siren gaze that she shortly covered with a voluminous smoke, his urges compelled him to squeeze her behind.

"Fifty bucks for a BJ", she casually said. He nodded and let her lead him to the side of a black dumpster. She knelt and unwrapped his blue jeans like a Christmas present as he frantically checked if anyone was around. Seeing that the coast was clear, he closed his eyes and paced himself for a *quick blow*.

She spat her gum and threw her cigarette on the ground. With gung-ho, she devoured his hairy and girthy yearning like a popsicle stick on a hot summer day.

"Mmm, mmm, mmm", she let out, giving her best performance to ensure that their quickie was as accurate as the word. Filling the alley with the sound of his chiming belt buckle, he grabbed her locks from the intensity of her oral embrace.

"Yeah, keep going, ahh".

Not wanting to kill the momentum, she commenced her flawless toothless performance and gave him a smooth ride. Unfortunately for her, he was much too insatiable that her mastery of penilingus paled in comparison to what he wanted out of her.

"Gwak!" she let out right after he impaled her throat without a warning. As his knees shook from the tactile delight, a stream of tears fell on her delicate cheeks.

"Ahhh! That's it, that's what you're looking for. You like it big don't cha?"

She pretended not to hear a word and continued sucking and sinking her scarlet-polished fingers into his butt. Briefly, he unhinged from her mouth and slapped her scarlet visage with his solid manhood.

"Fucking answer me! You like it, don't cha!?"

"Y-yes, yes!" she succumbed as she nodded her head like a troll.

"Good girl… ahh, there you go", he let out as soon as he was back in her oral embrace. Softly, he unhinged his grab from her locks, releasing the tension from her scalp then shortly trailed to her chest.

Perturbed by not feeling anything but the cushion of her black bra's foam under her white tank top, he squeezed some more. As he tried to insert his hands under her bra, she interlaced her fingers with his. However, her strength wasn't enough to mitigate his curiosity. Without thinking things through, he slid and felt her flat breasts.

"You!? You a *tranny*!?"

With a shiver down her spine, she shook her head and picked herself up from the ground.

"You fucking trap! Answer me!" he commanded as he raised her chin to check for an Adam's apple.

"Get off me!"

"No, you stay here! You cocksucking whore!"

"P-please… let me go. You d-don't have to pay me", she begged as he forced her cheek against the dumpster.

"Nobody plays with me, you understand!?"

Feeling his handgun's mouth graze her temples, all she could do was close her eyes and pray. As he pulled her shorts down with utmost aggression…

What the fuck!?

There he was, Brian, in his liquor-soiled black dress shirt and jeans, forced to lucidity from having witnessed the older man holding Honey at gunpoint.

In an utmost stealth effort, he took off his leather shoes and sauntered toward the man's back.

"Gah!" he screamed after successfully stealing the aggressor's gun. With eyes looking like they were about to fly off their sockets, she fell to the ground as she locked her sight on the random savior.

"Stay away from her!" he followed as he aimed at the man's head like his eyes had crosshairs.

"Haha! From him, you mean?"

"Come on, *mijo*, this is just some tranny slut, give me the gun".

"Stay the fuck away from her!"

"Give me the gun or I'll choke this *puta* to death", he sternly warned before pulling her by the hair and locking his arms around her neck.

Fuck...

"You don't know me, boy, I do whatever I say!"

He spat on the ground and suffocated her as he looked at the young man with a smug face. Seeing her struggle and run out of breath caused his knees to feel like *Jell-O*. With cold sweat that drenched his shirt and convulsive shivers, it was a miracle how his grip remained sturdy.

With the man's quick head bow brought upon the licking of his captive's face, Brian pulled the trigger.

Bang!

"Ahhh!" she screamed with a face painted with her captor's blood. As she quivered on the ground and wiped her face with her jacket, he regained consciousness.

Fuck!

"Fuck, fuck, fuck! What have I done!?" he let out as he stared at his bloody hands.

"Let's get out of here!" she suggested before

pulling his wrist with feminine vigor. As they rushed to the next alley where her black *Honda* touring bike was parked, the man spent his last breath reaching for his gun.

Chapter 2

*V*room! Vroom!*

Brian, still in disbelief at how he answered the conundrum, could do nothing but cling to Honey's waist. As the breeze blew her hair on his face and his nose was hit with the smell of her *Victoria's Secret Bombshell* perfume, the sillage of the man's blood still lingered harder.

"Thanks for saving me out there!" she yelled—fighting the speed of her bike to be audible.

"Where are we going?!"

"I know a place—where we could wash the blood off!"

No!

"Let's go to the police station! It was self-defense!"

Hearing the word police triggered her to accelerate the speed of her motorcycle.

"Slow down!"

"The police know that I'm a prostitute! They'll put both of us in jail!".

What the fuck!?

Briefly, he regretted his decision. He pondered that maybe the man wasn't sexually assaulting her. But witnessing how she almost choked to death, he had to be sure.

"Do you know that guy!?"

"No!"

"Why did he put his gun to your head!?"

"Maybe because he found out that I'm trans! I don't know!"

That's insane!

"Let's go to the police station! Maybe he's still alive!"

"I'm not taking that risk! I'll drop you off at the construction site! Do whatever you want!"

After an argumentative ride, there they were, in a public toilet at the construction site of a new Wynn Casino branch in Las Vegas. Feeling like ants were crawling all over his masculine body from utter disgust, he scrubbed his chest with his wet shirt on the sink like he was scrubbing the back of a frying pan.

After getting rid of every foreign scarlet pigment on his 5ft. 11in. frame, there she was, pristine and absent of any trace of the harrowing incident.

"Can you turn around?" she requested. Shortly after, she unhooked her bra to get rid of the blood.

"You must be regretting your decision. I mean, why save a prostitute? Right?"

Staring at the floor, all he could do was shake his head and listen.

"His choke… was real… and if you didn't arrive, he would've shot me after getting off."

"Hey…", he said, sinking his fingertips into her arms. Feeling embarrassed by him seeing her flat chest, she covered them with her wet bra.

"I don't regret it. Anyone would've done the same if they were in my position". With a scarlet face, she motioned him to look away before commencing rinsing her bra off any redness.

"I'm sorry but I can't go to the police station. They'll put me in the male prison".

"What about me?"

"They'll probably do the same, and you left the gun with your fingerprints and by the looks of it, your shoes", she answered as she stared at his feet that were insufficiently cushioned with black socks.

"Fuck! Fuck! Fuck!"

"I'm supposed to go to Harvard Law next month!"

Unsure of how to console him as her problems consisted of how to hide from the police, where to sleep, and get the meal from for the coming days, she giggled.

Huh!?

"You think this is funny!?"

"No…"

"It's just… you should be worrying about the police and not school".

With all her might, she wrung her bra and wore her damp attire. She took a hair tie from the pocket of her leather jacket and bit it as she fixed her hair in a bun.

"Where are you going?"

"Canada, probably, my life is over here. I know a guy in Minnesota that could help me cross the border".

With a heart beating a mile a minute, witnessing her treat the conundrum with utmost confidence amidst the impending repercussions provided him a sense of security. Being an only child, most of his decisions were planned out for him by his parents.

At that very moment, his lack of sound decision-making solidified when…

What the hell…

"Can I go with you?"

Feeling her heart fall to the pit of her stomach, she wanted to say no. She didn't like establishing connections with anyone, most especially when her parents disowned her when she came out as a transgender woman just a year ago. But knowing that there was a huge possibility of him, rotting in jail at a young age because of saving her... she nodded.

"Let's get you some shoes".

Chapter 3

"Where are we going?" Brian queried.

"We're gonna make some money", Honey nonchalantly said.

Vroom! Vroom!

The man's look, struggling on the ground kept creeping into his head and proved to be a good distraction to the novel feeling of riding a motorcycle at her heart-stopping driving pace. Albeit the majestic casino lights of the Las Vegas strip were aglow, his disposition remained dim.

He should be alive...

Moments later, there they were, by the fountain of the *Ceasars Palace*. Perturbed why they were hanging out at the center of the hotel right after shooting a stranger, he couldn't help but ask.

"What are we doing here?"

Gracefully, she blew the smoke from her cigarette and glanced at him. With her hair freshly dried from the speed of her bike, he started to appreciate how gorgeous the 29-year-old biker chick, particularly after seeing her with a calmer disposition.

"*Hoo*".

"This. I have a buyer already", she answered after showing him a 22-karat gold necklace with an angel pendant that she stole that night from another customer after taking it out of her leather jacket's pocket.

"If you're coming with me, you should sell your phone too… the police will track us with that thing", she followed after sliding into his jeans' pocket without permission.

"Honey! Hello, beautiful!" a masculine black man in a black suit ensemble in his early thirties greeted before planting a kiss on her cheek.

Honey?!

"Show me the goods".

"Damn! Someone got lucky tonight!"

"I'll take it for a grand".

"Fuck you, Will, you know how heavy that thing is".

"Oh, and this one too", she added before handing Brian's *iPhone 14 Pro Max* to him.

"Hmm, I don't know about this. I already have a lot of this shit. Hard to sell".

"Take it for three hundred bucks", she responded.

"Sweet!" Will exclaimed.

"What the fuck!? No, I'm gonna keep it!" Brian retaliated. Squeezing his arm, she leaned into his ear, sending a shiver down his spine.

"This is better than nothing. We have to get rid of it", she whispered.

Fine!

"Give me my sim card!"

"Relax bro. You don't have to yell".

"Honey, I'll give you two grand for everything. Take it or leave it".

"Why are you letting your boyfriend take advantage of you!? He's ripping you off!"

"Haha! Will? He's not my boyfriend".

"Then why does he call you Honey?!"

"Haha! That's her name, bro, chill. What's wrong with you?"

Oh...

"Two grand and a half, if you don't want it, I'm going to my contact in *Palms*". Knowing that he could easily sell the necklace for an easy five grand with the bonus of Brian's phone that he got dirt-cheap, Will succumbed.

"Damn, okay, okay, here".

Will took a wad of *Benjamins* out of his suit's pocket and licked the tip of his finger. As he counted the hundred dollar bills that were needed to close the deal, Brian's paranoia started creeping in.

They must be looking for me now...

"There you go". Shortly after, he detached his platinum brooch and used its pin to release Brian's sim card.

"And for you, grumpy", he followed as he surrendered the sim card to Brian.

"It was nice doing business, as usual. When are you gonna call me for pleasure, Honey baby?"

"Shut up, Will. Haha! Bye".

As Will happily went back to the casino, she lit up another cigarette.

She's like a chimney…

"This'll be enough if we're not careless with our spending. Dammit, if I knew that this would happen I wouldn't have blown everything last night in the Hyatt".

"You look loaded, even if you don't have shoes… you got some cash?"

"I don't use an ATM. I could get it later when the banks open".

"*Hoo…* no, can't take that risk, the police have probably alerted the banks right now. We better get going. Let me just finish this stick".

"Can't we wear the helmets this time?"

"No, we'll only do that when we get a decent

shower. I don't want that smell lingering on my bike. Don't worry, I'll go slower".

Shortly after, they started riding through the *Hoover Dam*. It helped him achieve his first mental break from the gruesome memory of shooting the man. His olfactory sense started getting used to the scent of his blood and at that very period, he began appreciating the sight of the Nevada-Arizona border.

"This looks so cool!" he exclaimed.

"Yes! Is it your first time!?"

"Yes!" he answered—as he marveled at the night lights that the gigantic dam offered. As the breeze blew on their faces, he turned to his left and glanced at the peaceful waters of the Colorado river. Albeit it didn't pose harm, his thalassophobia sent a shiver down his spine.

"How long have you been driving a motorcycle?!"

"Since I was twelve! You're safe with me!"

Maybe I am...

After saving her, it was his turn to be saved. However, he briefly pondered if she really had the capability of doing so when he was the one who offered her salvation to begin with. But at that very moment, riding with her, clinging to her waist, and letting her take the lead kept him going.

Over an hour later, just after the dawn rose, there they were, in the humble city of Kingman, Arizona. It was the second week of August and the mornings have become cooler—gearing towards fall. As his feet started feeling the repercussions...

"I can't wait to take a shower!" she said.

"Me too!"

As he curled his toes, there it was, *The Motelito*, a small-town motel with a maroon roof that was dressed in cracked paint that had two floors and twenty-two rooms.

The lobby was painted offwhite and dressed with photos of cowboys. Slowly, they inched their way to the sleeping tubby male receptionist in a tiki shirt.

Ding!

Interrupted by her bell ringing but still lulled, the man wiped the saliva from his mouth and attended to them.

"How much is it for one night?" she asked.

"Which kind of room?"

"What kind do you have?"

"Standard, Superior, Deluxe—".

"What does the standard room have?"

"A queen-sized bed, cable TV, WiFi, it doesn't have a tub though".

"No, that's fine. How much is it?"

"A hundred and fifty".

One-fifty for this shithole?

"That's too expensive", she softly retaliated.

"We give discounts if you stay longer. You can get the room for a hundred bucks a night if you stay for more than three days". Dying to meet with a bar of soap, she succumbed.

"That's fine. Here".

Moments later, there they were, in room 14B, settling in their stately bedroom decked in moss and olive. As soon as she arrived, she turned the television on.

There it was, the *Arizonian* morning news, reporting the hunt for Brian Bacall and Honey Jones. The police got Brian's information from the fingerprint that he left on the weapon and Honey's, from Will being interrogated as to why he had Brian's iPhone.

Fuck!

"Honey! We're on the news!"

With toothpaste in her mouth, she sprinted to the bedroom. It turned out that the man he shot was Luis Bautista, one of the top financial advisors at *Merrill Lynch*.

"Please, help us! If you find these criminals, inform the police. They must pay for what they've done to my husband", Lisa, Luis' wife tearfully pleaded in her blue terrycloth robe during a reporter's ambush interview.

Meanwhile, in the Bacall household, Mariana, Brian's mother, was clutching her white silk robe's collar as she tucked her blonde hair behind her ear. Tearful and in disbelief, she could do nothing but rest on her husband's chest as they witnessed the harrowing revelation on the TV that was hung in their bedroom decked in Renaissance luxury.

Back in room 14B...

Huh!?

Honey took Brian's shirt off without a warning. Feeling his heart beat a mile a minute, she took hers off as well, revealing her slender body with nothing on but a black bra and leather shorts.

"We should shower together to save time. The police are probably looking for us now!"

Oh...

Shortly after, there they were, Brian and his masculine body and girthy flaccid manhood that was dressed in a lush carpet of blonde pubic hair and Honey, with her soft candy stick, petite body, and flat chest, taking turns under the shower head. Like the clumsy and adventurous girl that she was, she accidentally dropped the soap.

Fucking hot...

As she picked it up, he was given a preview of her pink and tight balls and cleanly shaven orifice. Wanting to stop himself, he simply couldn't. Although Honey had a member, she looked quintessentially feminine. The novelty of a naked trans woman, who was only a hair away from him, introduced him to emotions he didn't know he had.

Fuck... I'm not gay...

Covering his boner in an effort not to scare her...

"Oh, haha! You must be happy to see me", she jested.

Shit!

"S-sorry", he softly let out with a scarlet face.

"Turn around", she nonchalantly said before she lathered his back gently. As she lathered his smooth back, he couldn't stop his circumcised *eight-incher* from twitching in a myriad of directions.

What the!?

"Oh!"

At that time, it was her turn to apologize. Her seven-inch *shecock* poked his right butt cheek without a warning from the uncontrollable effects of seeing the masculine man with a Loch Ness monster attached between his legs.

"Sorry about that", she gingerly said. It was the first time he heard her with a meek voice. Her usual speaking voice only consisted of two tones— nonchalance and command.

I can't take it anymore!

Without thinking things through, he turned

around and drew her to him then started locking lips with her.

"Is it okay…", he said with a pant.

At a loss for words and hypnotized by his sapphire eyes, she kissed him back and offered her minty tongue. With a heart that beat a mile a minute and with his stern heterosexuality on life support, he consumed her—discarding every worry on which porn category their naked first kiss belonged to.

So soft, so sweet…

"Mmm". "Mmmmm", he moaned back.

"Your lips are so soft, Honey…".

"Ahhh!" he let out after she lathered his boner with the soap. Wanting to relish his kisses, reality started creeping into her mind once more.

"Fuck! What are we doing!? We have to hurry!" she said.

At a frantic pace, they scrubbed each others' bodies—in a helpless effort that somehow, as they washed the stench of blood off their bodies, the memory of the night would soon wash away too.

Chapter 4

The coffee from The Motelito proved to be an authentic Colombian roast as two hours later, Honey was still up and running albeit having had no sleep from the previous night. Both in black helmets, their form of communication as they rode had to be thunderous exclamations.

"Where are we!?" Brian asked.

"Fuck!"

And just like that, she threw her cell phone on the road.

"Thanks for reminding me!"

She meant to throw her cell phone away but

their kisses distracted her. His question reminded her of GPS and was the perfect trigger to get rid of the tracker.

"We're close to Flagstaff!"

Originally, she wanted to take the route from Utah to Minnesota, but having more knowledge of obscure roads in New Mexico to mislead the police, she pivoted. Almost an hour more, there they were, in a little town in Winona, Arizona.

It was a chilly morning ten minutes past eight when they parked by *Heidi Ho's* novelty store.

"Welcome to Heidi Ho's", a middle-aged woman in an orange vest greeted.

In the store with log walls that proudly housed rows of cowboy gear, party favors, and beef jerky, his view of her womanhood was solidified as he stared at her exhibition of stereotypical indecisiveness.

The women's clothing section barely had variety but she couldn't choose between a white v-neck t-shirt and a white round-collared tank top.

"I finally got the shoes", he said, holding a $200 pair of brown leather cowboy boots.

"We can't afford that", she whispered.

Having been brushed with a financial problem for the very first time, he obliviously took the cheapest footwear that he could get, a pair of rubber slippers that were two for three bucks.

"Seriously? Do you wanna freeze to death?"

"You told me that we can't afford the shoes".

"We can't afford the ones you've got. Take something below a hundred bucks".

Moments later, there they were, by the cash register, her with five pieces of white tank tops, a pink thermal jacket, five pairs of jean shorts, and a pair of high-heeled lucite stilettos.

That's odd...

"Don't you have clothes in your trunk?"

"I do. Please take that—over there", she answered with a request as she pointed at a straight long blonde wig on a mannequin head by the door.

"That'll be $314, plus fifty for the wig".

"Here you go, mam".

A little later, as they stopped to get some gas from a nearby *Shell* station, she opened the box of her bike with utmost elation as they ate hotdogs on a yellow metal patio.

"I know that you might find this crazy but, these are yours", she said, with the blonde wig and pink jacket in tow.

What the fuck?!

"Not gonna happen", he let out before taking another bite of the mustard-filled delight.

"What's so wrong about it?"

"Haha! Stop pretending like you don't know".

Perturbed as she brushed the synthetic fibers of the wig, she leaned closer to get a better answer.

"I'm not gay".

Oh…

With the insensitive remark that ate him up, he swallowed a huge chunk of hotdog along with his words.

"You know what I mean…".

Looking like the nerves on her temples were about to pop, she scratched her scalp as she stared blankly at her unfinished food.

"Being gay is the last thing you should be worrying about!"

Fuck...

With intent and a tearful gaze, she faced him head-on.

She kicked the metal foot of the square table—sending a shiver down his spine.

"You and I are gonna be put in jail for until who knows when!? You're lucky to have a family! Mine kicked me out and I'll probably rot there as a prison bitch for the rest of my life!"

"What don't you fucking understand!?"

And just like that, as the first tear fell on her cheek, he held her from the back and kissed her head.

"I'm sorry, I'm sorry, shh... everything's gonna be alright...".

Knowing that he too was unsure of his presumptions and still half-hearted about wearing feminine clothing...

"I'll do it, I'll do it", he followed.

Slowly, she faced him and drenched his black dress shirt with her tears—questioning why her life turned out the way it was.

We won't get caught... I promise...

"I'm sorry that you had to get involved in my shitty life...".

"Shh, shh, it was my choice to protect you".

"I'll keep protecting you... I promise...".

No man has treated her with utmost chivalry and Brian was the redemption that she had been waiting for. But with a twist of fate, she got exactly what she prayed for, in all the wrong places and at the very wrong time.

However, at that moment, with his strong arms as her cushion and his warm breaths as the music to her ears, she couldn't have asked for something better. With utmost gratitude, she looked up and returned his promise with a saccharine kiss.

Chapter 5

After an arduous nine-hour journey from Winona, Arizona, there they were, just before seven in the evening in the *Palo Duro Canyon State Park* in New Mexico, City. Honey had to traverse to what was often dubbed the mini *Grand Canyon* of Texas as she knew that staying in a crowded city like Amarillo would get them into trouble.

It was past nine in the evening and two bottles of Budweiser beer were all she needed to fall asleep. As she wandered off to dreamland in their dingey orange bedroom in room 3C at the *Motel 74*, Brian couldn't help but gaze at her peaceful visage.

Her sun-kissed skin, the long brown locks that rested chaotically on the white pillow, the feminine features of her small face that looked more passable without makeup, and her tight body with nothing but black cotton panties on, were all too inviting for him not to take notice.

Knowing that she was exhausted, he didn't dare to make a slight movement that could compromise her much-needed rest. Stealthily, he removed his clothes and took a hot shower.

Huh...

The next morning proved to be one of the best days of his life. It was just ten minutes before nine when his restful slumber was disrupted by a warm and wet awakening. As he relished his vivid wet dream, he slowly opened his eyes.

There she was, licking his morning wood in a myriad of directions.

"Good morning", she briefly let out.

"Ahhh", he moaned—in disbelief and utmost happiness.

"Fuck yeah, keep going...".

Every fiber of his body felt like they were

being electrocuted by an orgasmic jolt. Her tongue flicks were swift, her suctions were tight, and the way she squeezed his balls was gentle yet palpably mindblowing.

"I couldn't help it. Having you next in bed with me with just those skimpy white briefs... ugh".

"Mmm, mmm, mmm".

"Fuck!" he let out in utter delight right after she impaled her throat with his hairy *eight-incher.*

"Gwak!"

"Honey... you're gonna make me cum so fast...".

As soon as she had a taste of the premature bubble that he squirted, she unhinged her mouth and started kissing him. Feeling her hard nipples graze against his chest made his dick twitch uncontrollably.

Her tuck started hurting as she too was getting hot and bothered. While keeping his mouth locked with hers, she discreetly unleashed her *shecock* from her thighs. As she let it rest inside her black panties —pointing in the 12 o'clock direction, he started feeling her solidity.

Fuck...

Seeing her hard for him when they showered together already piqued his curiosity, but feeling her boner carelessly rub against his skin only intensified his yearning to discover his sexuality.

"Ah!" she let out, after he cupped her boner, causing her to squirt a bubble of pink venom on his hand.

"You don't have to do that".

But I want to...

Softly, he jerked her cock and circled her precum with his index finger. As she rolled her head in euphoria, he gazed at her and let her witness how much he wanted her. Slightly, he opened his mouth and tasted her *ladygravy*.

Sweet...

As she watched him lick his fingers with a lascivious gaze, she had to liberate herself. Slowly, she stood up and rolled her panties down, giving him a point of view of her sturdy lady penis that was begging to be sucked.

She sat on his chest, causing her mushroom head to poke his neck. Shortly after, she circled her hand on his shaft as he fed himself with his thick finger.

I can't take it anymore!

Try as he might, having tasted her precum killed every stern heterosexual thought in his mind. As he circled her mouth with his finger, he leaned closer and started licking her moist mushroom head.

"Ahhh!" she moaned.

"I haven't done this before...".

"Just think of it as a huge clit".

She continued by jerking his extra-solid manhood as he started consuming half of her dick.

This isn't so bad...

Having only half of her shaft felt like torture. Slowly but surely, she moved closer and inserted every inch of her dick in his virgin mouth.

"Gwak!" she let out as soon as her mushroom head knocked on his tonsils.

"Fuck! Your mouth's so warm!"

"Gwak! Gwak!"

Being a novice, he was unsure if what he was doing was right—but seeing her shiver like she was having a convulsion made him feel like he just earned a master's degree in penilingus.

"Mmm! Am I as sweet as honey?"

He nodded like a troll with a tearful face as he endured her fervor. Albeit having a hard time to breath, he had no qualms as the novel flavor kept feeding every desire that he never knew he had.

Seeing her gorgeous face and voluminous wilful hair from her flips while taking her erection made him feel like he was the harbinger of her pleasure. Proudly, he breathed harder through his nose, swallowing his saliva and her every premature secretion.

"Gwak!"

"I'm close!"

"Mmm!" he let out a guttural groan.

"Brian! I'm cumming!"

Yes, cum for me!

"Ahh!"

"Mmm!"

"Gwah!"

"Mmmmm!"

"Ah! Ahh! Ahhh!"

And just like that, she released her thick and creamy joy juice in his virgin passage.

So thick...

As her *babygravy* freely trailed down his throat, he felt like he just had a spoonful of warm honey. With her penis still hard, she unhinged from him and tasted herself through his mouth.

"Mmm, thanks, Brian".

"You taste so good, as sweet as Honey".

"It's your turn", she said giggly. Shortly after, she lubricated his erection with her saliva.

"Ahhh", he let out from her wet and gentle hand strokes.

"I've never had something this big in my life", she followed with utmost excitement.

"You don't have to, Honey".

"Why shouldn't I? This is like winning the jackpot".

Pacing herself, she squeezed her face in anticipation.

"Fuck!" she yelled after only having consumed

two inches of him.

"I'm sorry", he gingerly said.

With a faint smile, she shook her head. His manhood wasn't to be dealt with lightly. Not only was it long, but it was also veiny, girthy, and extra solid. After subsequent panting, she challenged herself once more.

"Ugh!" she followed after halfway through his tower.

"You're so damn big…".

"Gahhh!"

Fuck!

And just like that, she felt what it was like to partake in the reverse taking of the Excalibur, and it was also his first time to experience what it was like for his penis to be embraced by the goddess of orgasm. As she rested her butt on his hairy thighs, she took his hands and motioned for him to play with her flat chest.

"Mmm, that's it", she encouraged after feeling him tweak her highly sensate pink nipples. Softly, he licked his index fingers and grazed her pointers —causing them to erect like they never had before from the tactile sensations of his saliva and the edge of his fingernails.

As she clenched her anal muscles—he felt as if he was being tortured from not being able to slide in and out of her extra tight and warm confinement. Soon after, as they both gazed at each other with utmost lasciviousness, every orgasmic beat from his penis started providing her prostate with pleasurable sensations.

"Mmm", she coquettishly moaned as she circled her hips, offering him a mindblowing feeling.

"This is so tight. Fuck Honey, I'm gonna cum so fast with this".

"Control yourself".

Slowly, she bobbed up and down, minding her pace to make sure he didn't cum too fast. With a scarlet face and his eyes looking like they were about to fly off their sockets, he curled his toes in an effort to suppress his orgasm.

Fuck! Fuck! Fuck!

Sinking his fingertips on her hips, she started getting hard again, turning him on even further. She wanted to control her rhythm but she needed to feel another poke on her prostate.

"Ah!" she let out.

"Honey!"

She tied her hair with her hands and continued jumping up and down—giving him the most intense sensations that he hasn't felt before. He couldn't do anything but roll his head and close his eyes in euphoria.

Curling his toes once more, every tight brushing of her walls of pleasure—suffocating his girthy penis, made him briefly wish that the feeling wouldn't stop.

"Fuck! I'm close!"

"Ahh! Me too!" she said as she stroked her cock while riding his dick.

"Fuck! Honey!"

"You're so fucking tight!"

"Ahh! Gahhh!"

"Brian!"

However, his wish wasn't granted as the limits of his body started overtaking. In a deliriously delicious disposition, he curled his toes again and sunk his fingertips on her hips tighter as he exploded an abundance of thick and warm cum in her tight ass.

"Whooo!" he let out as the nerves on his neck look like they were about to pop.

"I'm cu—", she followed after releasing a puddle of clear lady liquid on his belly. Both exhausted and relishing their orgasms, she squeezed her anal muscles once more, ensuring that she milked him dry.

"Man... this is crazy!" he let out.

"You're so good", she followed as she satietedly sat on top of his hard penis. Moments later, as he started losing virility, she unhinged and rested on his sweaty chest.

"I thought you wouldn't like it".

Hmmm...

"Why not?"

"Yesterday, with the wig, I just felt like you weren't comfortable".

With a gentle smile, he planted a kiss on her forehead.

"I don't know. I guess you have the power to make me do the things that I don't want to do".

Overwhelmed with his acceptance, all she could do was rub her face against his chest and hope that the brief moment that they were sharing wouldn't last.

Chapter 6

Maybe it was infatuation, maybe he was smitten, or maybe just like Honey, Brian was starting to develop something that felt out of place at a very critical stage of his life, maybe, he was falling in love, he pondered.

As he cultivated the possibilities in his head while lathering his penis with the hotel's *Irish Spring* soap bar, she entered the bathroom that was surrounded by maroon tiles without a warning.

"Hey sexy", she said as she scoured through the basket of free toiletries atop the white counter. Shortly after, there she was, with a yellow razor and a bottle of conditioner in tow.

"The disguise starts today".

Covering his face from the embarrassing feeling of dressing up as a woman, she knelt and started lathering his legs with conditioner.

"Turn it off".

As soon as the water's resonance faded, he started enjoying the view of her naked back and the silky feeling of hair conditioner on his legs.

"Don't they have shaving cream?"

"Uh-uh. Don't worry, this will work just as fine".

Crunching noises started filling the room from each careful glide with the razor.

"Sadly, we have to get rid of this. Dammit!" she informed, regretting the activity as she had a huge body hair fetish. After tapping the accumulated blonde hair on the floor, she stood up and started tickling his armpits.

"Haha! Stop it!"

With a frown, she motioned for him to lift his arms. Like a rabid tigress, she sniffed the hairy nook like she was about to devour her prey.

"Buh-bye babies".

"Aww, don't be sad, I grow them back easily".

She gently applied conditioner to his armpits and started shaving away his carpet of testosterone-induced growth. Once done, she examined his face underneath the bright white light.

"Damn, didn't realize you were such a pretty boy", she jested as she caressed his face.

Albeit she complimented him in a playful way, he was indeed a pretty boy. Natural blonde locks, magnetic sapphire eyes with tinges of gray, a short and slim nose, a small face, and compact yet round and full lips, were all too delicate-looking for a full-grown man.

Carefully, she started ridding him of his errant mustache and beard before kissing his yearning lips. Shortly after, he sauntered in front of the bathroom's mirror and gazed at his hairless face and armpits.

"I feel lighter".

"Yeah, freshly shaven is a nice feeling, wait till they start growing back, it'll feel like itchy hell haha".

Fuck!

After a hot shower together, there he was, staring at the outfit that she has prepared for him on the white mattress. A pink thermal jacket, a white tank top, a pair of jean shorts, and a nylon black bra and panty combo.

"I don't know how to wear this", he said as the bra dangled on his arm.

"This is gonna be a little tight on you but it'll make you look like you have tits".

"Oomph!"

"Yea, sorry about that", she said after hooking the straps at the back.

Restricted and irritated, he inserted a foot in the hole of the panty that she stretched for him. Once both of his legs were in place, she asked him to straddle in preparation for the tucking.

No!

"That's gonna hurt!"

"Brian... you have a monster dick. How are we gonna remain stealth if people keep gawking at your bulge?"

Dammit!

"I don't even know how to…".

Softly, she walked to his back and pulled his member—letting everything rest at the back of his thighs.

"Close your legs".

She then rolled the panties up—pulling them as high as she could to ensure that he had a flat crotch.

"It feels weird", he let out as he pressed his hand against the smooth flat surface of his nylon panties.

"You'll get used to it".

Moments later, there he was, gazing at the novel sight of himself with a blonde wig on and a biker chick ensemble.

"Woah! I look kinda hot".

The pink jacket successfully hid his girthy arms and helped hugely in creating a passable illusion. His torso looked femininely delectable as it was absent of belly flab and his hairless masculine thighs looked like they were begging to be spread in his denim short shorts. The boots that he bought didn't go exactly with the whole ensemble but they were able to hide his bulky calves.

"Pucker up", she requested as she darted the

blunt crayon of her red lipstick at his lips.

"Do I have to wear makeup?"

"Girls who wear slutty shorts put in the effort. You have to look the part".

So smooth…

As he relished the novel buttery feeling of wearing lipstick, the uncomfortable feeling of having a restricted penis started creeping in, and at that moment, his respect for her elevated.

"Wait for it!" she exclaimed.

"Now, that's hot!" she followed after covering his eyes with a pair of black aviators.

"I look like a bad girl".

Playfully, she squeezed his butt, causing him to lean in for a kiss.

"Uh-uh! Lipstick…", she retorted.

It was fifteen minutes before ten in the morning as the Texan sunshine beamed on their glorious bodies just outside of the Motel 74.

"Look at that!" he exclaimed as he marveled at the sight of the Palo Duro canyon.

"Is that even real?"

"Yeah, from erosions. I'd like to take you there but we don't have time", she answered—peering with him and basking in the view of the 120-mile canyon's glory.

Carefully, he wore the black helmet on top of his wig.

"Make sure it's extra tight, we only have one wig".

"You good now?" she followed.

As he clung his arms around her waist, his ass proved to be a distraction for the vehicles that were about to trail them. Unsure if he was passable but sure of his trust for her, he held tight.

Vroom! Vroom!

"This is amazing!" he said—referring to the abundant rows of canyons and steep hills.

"Yeah! Nothing you can find in the city!"

Albeit having ridden her bike numerous times— the novelty of journeying with her still hasn't died down. Each day was a new adventure, each hour was a new view, and each minute was a new feeling.

Might as well...

"I love you!" he said as they rode through a steep hill.

"What!? I didn't hear that!"

"I wanna scream it on the mountain top! I love you!"

"I love you, Honey Jones!"

"Ha ha ha!"

"Whooo!" he said—lifting his arms.

"Don't let go! Crazy!" she let out in exasperation as she slowed down from his brief exhibition of foolery.

"Say you love me too or I'll let go!" he cheekily demanded.

"Crazy!"

"Say it! Say it!" he egged—loosening his grip on her waist.

"I love you too! Brian Bacall!"

"Muah! Muah! Muah!"—planting her shoulder with profuse kisses as butterflies swarmed in his belly.

A little over ten hours later, there they were, in *Gretna*, a small city just before Omaha, Nebraska. As the twilight started coming alight with the help of the bright lights of the small establishments, there it was, *Capitol 7 Casino*, in neon green—a blinding distraction that caused her to pull over.

"I have to smoke", she said.

"Go ahead, Honey bunny", he *slutilly* jested as he sat beside a cactus by the two-story mini-casino.

As she puffed away her exhaustion, she mentally calculated the amount of money they had left.

"*Hoo*. We're running out of money. We should probably try our luck".

No!

"Are you insane?!" There should be another way".

"Don't start with a negative mindset. That's unlucky".

"I'll give my friends a phone call".

"*Hoo*. Look, the moment that your face appeared on their TV screens is the same moment when they stopped becoming your friend".

"I'm not gonna blow everything. Just trust me".

Having been taken care of thus far, he couldn't do anything but succumb.

"I'll keep half our money just in case".

"Deal".

With a little over four hundred bucks in her hand and roughly the same amount in his leather jacket, they started strolling the small room decked in red velvet and smelled like cigarette smoke.

As she determined the slot machine that would multiply their money, he couldn't stop cringing from the novel feeling of being objectified by middle-aged men. His pink ensemble glowed brightly under the faint yellow fluorescence of the humble casino. For a brief moment, his apparition paused their frustrated slaps against the buttons of their losing machines.

Moments later, their hundred dollars increased threefold from lucky free spins.

"Let's cash out!" he encouraged with a heart that didn't skip a beat.

"Shh. We're just getting started, this thing is lucky", she reassured as she tapped the side of the blue slot machine.

Two hours have gone and as the machine consumed all of her bills, he started dozing off on the other machine. As he took a nap, there he was, a sly young man in a black hoodie, checking Brian's consciousness from a distance.

With utmost swiftness, he inserted his hand and took the remaining cash that was peeking from the side of his pink jacket's pocket then rushed to the exit door.

"Brian", she softly said—as her guilt ate her up from throwing their money away.

"I'm done, let's buy some soda then go".

Still wiping the saliva off his face, he followed. As they waited to pay for their drinks on the counter, he dug deep into his pockets.

"Fuck! Did you take the rest of the cash?" he queried with a scarlet visage.

"Huh! I wouldn't ask to buy drinks if I took it from you. Just keep checking".

With profuse palpitations from the novel experience of not having the money to pay for two cans of Coca-Cola.

This is embarrassing...

"Mam!?" the middle-aged cashier in a green uniform impatiently asked. Annoyed by the unnecessary hustle as there were no other customers, she placed the soda cans on the counter and helped dig into his pockets.

"This is the only place I put it in!"

"Fuck! Fuck! Fuck!"

"We'll find it later. Let's go".

Moments later, there they were, staring blankly at each other on the ground beside her motorcycle.

"God! I'm so dumb!" she let out after kicking the wheel of her bike.

"Stupid slot machine!"

"Shh, shh", he let out softly as he brushed her back in consolation. As she drenched his pink jacket with her tears, his stomach started rumbling.

"Haha! I heard that".

Both tired, hungry, and thirsty, all they could do was let out a hearty laugh.

"We better get outta here", she informed after noticing a police car.

Ten miles away from the casino, they found

a spot where an oppressive oak tree was proudly erected. With no money, no food, and just enough gas for another hour, they decided to spend the night under it.

"Just stay close to me, we'll figure something out tomorrow", he said as she gently rested on his chest.

"I love you, Honey".

"I love you too, Brian".

Chapter 7

It was the same night and a little over eleven in the evening. Their only resolve was the warmth that the Nebraskan summer night offered. With nothing but their bodies hinged with a loving embrace, there it was, a police car, waking them up with its glaring headlamps.

"Everything good here? Mams?" a masculine Nebraskan police officer queried as he lusted over their scantily-clad bodies. As they softly nodded and peered, he rubbed his girthy neck in an effort to release his tension.

He inched closer to check their faces—causing his erection to grow even further. Brushing his brunette hair with one hand to the back of his head, he took a cigarette from his pocket with the other.

"Why are you gals sleeping here?" he said in a muffled tone.

"We're just… camping, sir".

With a smug look, he lit his cigarette and shook his head.

"*Hoo*. Not every night's a lucky night. But I can change that for you gals", he said as he rubbed the boner from his cream slacks.

Fucking pervert!

"I got fifty bucks for two mouths and another fifty for two pussies. *Hoo*".

Feeling protective of his new girlfriend and freshly knowledgeable about sucking cock, he let his desperation take over his body.

"She can't, she's tired tonight. I—I'll do it", he mildly retorted in his best attempt at a feminine voice.

"Okay blondie, but before we begin, I need to inspect what's in that box. You know, standard procedure".

As they sauntered to her vehicle, she couldn't help but voice out her trepidation.

"Just let me do it. It's gonna be quick".

"You're my girlfriend now, I can't let you suck someone else's dick!"

"Ugh! You're so old-fashioned!"

Curious about their bickering, he walked toward them, brightening her bike's tail box with a flashlight.

"Oomph, look at those sexy shoes. Wear them for me while you suck my cock".

Dammit!

Moments later, there he was, kneeling on the earthy ground—barely breaking into his girlfriend's 5-inch lucite heels. With utter excitement, the police officer dropped his pants and started impaling his mouth with his girthy and hairy *eight-incher*.

"Gwak!" he let out with a tearful face as she nervously watched from a distance.

"Ahh! A real cocksucker!"

"Ggg, ggg", he let out guttural groans from his careless thrusts.

"That's it, put it all in your throat".

"You like it don't you!?"

"Ahh!"

"Gwak!"

"Mmm, yeah!"

"I can't believe I'd go this low but fuck—keep sucking my cock you whore!"

Fuck you!

Feeling the officer's gung-ho by the way he was manhandling his face, he squeezed his butt in retaliation

"Fuck! You're a man!" the officer yelled in exasperation with the detached wig in his hand.

Without thinking things through, Brian let his primal instinct take control of his body—causing him to snatch the officer's *Glock 19* from the ground.

"Hands up!"

"Brian!" she yelled—freshly remembering the harrowing night when she witnessed him lose control. With only his adrenaline working, he intently pointed the gun at the pantsless officer.

"Get his radio, cellphone, money, everything!"

he commanded.

"Brian? Yeah, Brian Bacall! The fugitive duo that killed the Latino man in Vegas!"

"Shut up! Make one wrong move and I'll shoot!"

Having gone through shooting lessons, he released the pistol's safety, letting the officer know that he wasn't bluffing.

"I won't! Take everything!"

"Throw the radio and the phone".

Bang!

Bang!

Seeing the electronic shards fly in a myriad of directions caused the officer to lose his erection. As his sweat trickled down his neck, Brian liberated his feet from the heels and stepped into his boots once more.

Vroom! Vroom!

"You're crazy!" she exclaimed.

"Whoo!" he said with the wig in his hand and the officer's gun in the other.

Albeit not in the most likable circumstance, it was the very first time that he felt truly alive.

Most of his life was spent following his parents' plans, conforming to his friends, and doing things according to what everyone in his bubble deemed right.

She may have been disowned by her family for living as a woman, but he had been living in a gilded cage that he built himself.

The moon didn't shine brightly that night. It was just the breeze from the speed of her driving and her motorcycle's headlights that served as guides to their next destination.

As they basked in their freedom through the verdant and mountainous view of the *Chalco Hills*, he grabbed her tighter, clinging as he had never clung before.

"We'll get out of this mess soon!" he reassured.

"We just gotta keep going!" she seconded.

Suddenly… an influx of sirens started filling the area.

And just like that, it was the ending of their short-lived victory.

They failed to check the alarm attached to the bottom of the police officer's vehicle.

Dammit!

"Stop the vehicle, Honey Jones!" a male police officer announced through a megaphone.

"What are we gonna do!?"

Being chased by the police cars and rattled by her boyfriend's anxiety was the first time that she felt like she lost control. Not knowing what to do, she accelerated.

Grabbing her waist tighter, she kept going, in hopes that there was a force that could emancipate them.

"Slow down!"

However, when two more police cars intercepted them, she started losing hope. Unsure of what to do next, she accelerated.

"You're about to reach a dead-end. Stop your vehicle right now!"

Fuck!

"I'm gonna keep going! I'm gonna drop you off here!"

"Are you insane!? You're gonna die!"

"You have a life waiting for you! This is the end

for me!"

"There's no life without you! Take me with you!"

As the breeze dried her tears at a rapid pace, she couldn't bring herself to cause his demise. Determined to win at least once in her life by not getting caught, she slowed down and parked her bike.

"I'm gonna love you forever", she softly said—giving him a deep kiss.

No no no!

"Don't do this!"

The police cars started covering all bases. All she could see was the inviting vastness of *Wherspann Lake*. With feminine vigor, she pushed him out of her vehicle.

"Honey!"

Vroom! Vroom!

After one last look, she started moving.

Forgive me...

Without thinking things through, he targeted the wheels of her bike like his eyes had crosshairs.

Bang!

<h1 style="text-align:center">Chapter 8</h1>

oney only suffered from a minor concussion and superficial wounds. She got sent to a private cell in a male prison as soon as she recovered. The updates of the trial for the criminal case of Luis Bautista became the daily headline of news outlets.

Not being able to talk face-to-face with each other while regularly being in the presence of one another in the same courtroom felt like torture.

Brian's family hired the best lawyers and to Honey's surprise, her mother started connecting with the Bacall family in defense of her case. Seeing Honey behind bars and knowing that she wouldn't have worked as a prostitute if they only accepted her earlier, enveloped her with guilt.

Having a novel mother-and-daughter relationship, she doubled up as Brian and Honey's messenger—exchanging their sweet nothings through her.

It was the last day of the trial and Honey started losing hope. Rumors have been circulating that the public was on Luis' side. Nobody believed their claim of self-defense from sexual assault and attempted murder as the weapon used was owned by the victim. After all, the man had a clean record and the two of them were dubbed as thief prostitutes in drag.

Moreover, Brian's brief outdoor fellatio for the Nebraskan police officer only cemented the plaintiff's claim. Amidst the darkness that surrounded them that night at the oak tree, the road had discreet night vision cameras in place.

"Your honor, I'd like to say something", Luis' fourteen-year-old daughter Lena, interjected as the plaintiff's lawyer interrogated Brian.

As her mother, Lisa gasped at her daughter's audacity, and the members of the public started forgetting that their jaws had joints, their lawyer Bruce Gordon took over the microphone once more.

"Objection, your honor! Let me finish my questions".

"Objection overruled. Let her speak".

"What are you doing *mijita*!?" her mother queried with bulging eyes.

"With a tearful face, she inched to their lawyer's microphone".

"He—she… Honey, wasn't the only victim of my father. Me and my best friends as well. He is not a good man… I'm sorry *mami*".

And just like that, her mother held her as tight as she could. She had an inkling that it was happening but couldn't bring herself to believe that her husband would do the unthinkable to his own blood.

Moments later, Lena handed her phone with the videos that she recorded discreetly using her phone whenever he'd knock into her room.

An hour later, after witnessing the gruesome revelation, Lisa withdrew the case. She knew that pursuing Brian and Honey along with the new evidence and witnesses would just tarnish her family's reputation further. Instead, she decided to pursue the healing of her daughter's trauma.

And just like that, after the barriers of the trial vanished, Brian and Honey rushed to each other in their orange uniforms. From seeking metaphorical freedom to literal emancipation, there they were, without words and only brimming with longing and love.

"Thank you for setting me free...", she whispered.

"No... thank you, for showing me what real freedom is", he said back.

Epilogue

A year later, Brian started studying law. He realized that after what just happened to them, he needed to start with something that could take him to change the laws protecting women from all walks of life.

With Honey's passion for fast vehicles, she became a social media influencer and was able to grow her following to more than two million in just a month.

They shared a one-bedroom apartment close to his university in Boston and adopted a female cat that they named Brianna, after Brian's disguise. The people who once judged them started treating them like heroes.

Honey was completely happy with how their

life was. Little did she know, Brian was taking motorcycle driving courses in his free time. He planned to propose to her after taking her on a joy ride back to Palo Duro.

The End <3

Did you enjoy Joy Ride? In that case, I hope you could check out my first bundle Romantic Sissies Volume One.

It contains three sissification and feminization stories brought upon by domineering transgender women. In it, you will get six titillating books from the heart.

First Feminization Fiction - Modeling for Mrs. Morningwood

The first title follows the story of Danny, a lanky

high school senior who succumbs to a first-time feminization transformation brought upon by his first love for Mrs. Morningwood, a transgender woman who runs an adult publishing business.

Mrs. Morningwood finds out that Danny offered more than being a stand-in model. He reminds her that there was more to life than enduring a relationship with a cheating husband.

Second Feminization Fiction – Tokyo Sissy Hostess

The second title follows the story of Louie Liddledich, a travel vlogger who was determined not to take another dime from his wealthy father to pursue his passions. After several careless financial decisions, he stumbles upon a chance meeting with a Japanese transgender mama-san and loanshark who owns Tokyo's top sissy hostess club.

Discover how Louie swallowed his pride, ego, masculinity, and more *wink* in this forced feminization transformation and sissy training story.

Third Feminization Fiction – The Fifth Wife

The third title follows the story of Ahmed Al-Haziz, a multimillionaire tech magnate from a family of sheikhs in Dubai. With Amanda Cruz, his Asian transgender girlfriend's bubbling-up frustration from being treated like a holiday girlfriend, he was determined to prove her love to her by adhering to several conditions.

Amanda soon finds out that she bit more than she could chew after finding out that traveling to a middle-eastern country as a transgender woman was not exactly like a yellow cab ride. Just how will they be able to live as lesbian lovers with Ahmed's four wives and Amanda's immigration challenges in this sissy husband book?

Read Romantic Sissies Volume One

It encapsulates five titillating reluctant feminization stories of men submitting to sissification brought upon by domineering t-girls and femdom.

Read Top T-Girls and Sub Sissies

It encapsulates three transgender romance and MM stories of three sissies' forced feminization fairy tales with dominant transgender women, *futas*, and romantic gentlemen.

Read Sissy Fairy Tales
Volume One

Transformed By T-Girls Volume One is Lilly Lustwood's first collection of her Prima Femina Romances books.

Read Transformed By T-Girls Vol. One

Yearning to feel what it was like to be coveted as a lady, she secretly wrote her wishes in her songbook. On Christmas eve, the choirmaster stumbled upon her musings, then shared every detail from cover to cover... with her choirmates.

Read Oh! Carol – Coveted By The Choir

Underneath her pencil skirt and silk blouse, distracting all the yearning men in the conference room with her apparition, she knew exactly who to give her attention to for her next career opportunity.

Read The Office Gurl

Find a place with utmost privacy and join Lilly as she takes you back to 2007 when she experienced being coveted, objectified, and loved for the very first time.

Read My Cherry No More

"Vicious and criminally sexy, that's how they describe Stacey. Just how many notches on her bedpost should she accumulate to satiate her worldly desires?"

Read Stacey The School Sissy

"In an underground T-Girl Brothel lies the dreams of transgender women, only to find out that they were all disillusions. Will her newfound beauty and bravery emancipate her sisters from the harrowing confinement?"

Read Beauty In The Brothel

Author's Message

Dear Romantic Reader,

Thank you very much for purchasing and reading *Joy Ride – A Reluctant Feminization and T-Girl Suspense Romance.*

For a writer, I can't seem to find the best word to describe how grateful I am for your support.

If you enjoyed this book, KINDLY (with puppy-dog eyes) give it a Rating and Review it on Kindle.

Let's get it to the overall bestseller list <3

Should you feel the need to send me a message concerning this book, your love life, or just about anything, please feel free to follow the pages below and Subscribe to my Mailing List to get updates on Free Books, Promos, and New Releases.

Mailing List (stats.sender.net/forms/er756a/view)

Home Page (www.lillylustwood.wordpress.com)

Amazon Page (www.amazon.com/Lilly-Lustwood/e/B0B9X11BMR/)

Facebook | Twitter | TikTok (@LillyLustwood)

Goodreads (www.goodreads.com/lillylustwood)